With thanks to the children of Year 3, Ysgol y Graig, Llangefni.

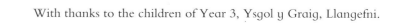

Alison and the
bully monsters

Jac Jones

PONT

First Impression—2000

ISBN 1 85902 752 0

This book is published with the support of an 'Arts for All' National Lottery grant from the Arts Council of Wales.

CRONFA LOTERI
LOTTERY FUND

Cover Design: Olwen Fowler

Printed in Wales at
Gomer Press, Llandysul, Ceredigion SA44 4QL.

Alison Little hardly ever went out.

"Why don't you go out to play, Alison?"
asked her mother.
"I just want to finish this story," she said.

"You should be outside enjoying the sunshine," her father said.

"I don't want to. I'd rather watch television," answered Alison.

"Why don't you take those big feet outside Wallyson!" growled her brother.

"Because I have to tidy my room," she replied. "Anyway, I don't have to go out if I don't want to."

"Well, you'll have to play outside today," said her mother. 'Things are going to get very busy in here. See you dinner time."

The dog next door barked and snarled at her. She stepped off the pavement and walked in the road. She always did.

Just down the road was Number Six, with the untidy garden. The boy came out and said he wanted her coloured bouncy ball.

And he took it.

Around the corner, a gang of bigger girls pushed her into a hedge and called her names. They stole Donna Duck and ran away, quacking and laughing.

Alison went to a lonely place. She felt sick, as though she had heavy stones in her tummy. When she felt like this she usually cried. It was always the same. But this time she didn't.

This time she was angry.

"Bullies!" she muttered.

"Monsters!" she shouted.

"Bully Monsters!" she screamed.

"What?" said a voice behind her.

"What?" said another voice, like an echo.

Alison spun round.

"Who are you?" she gasped.

"We're Bully Monsters!" they shouted as one.

Alison's anger flared again.
"Well, I don't like being bullied, and I'm fed up with it," she shouted back at them.

"But it's what we do best," said one.
"It's what we're good at," said the other.

"Well it's not the best, and it isn't any good.
It's just cruel," said Alison fiercely.

"I'm sorry," said the Bully Monster.
"So is he," said the other one.

Alison didn't feel so angry now. She looked at the surprised faces of the Bully Monsters.

"You can come to my house for some ice cream if you want to," she said.

She felt happy, and happy felt nice.

These were two new friends, big friends, who would help her to get back her coloured bouncy ball and Donna Duck.

"Give me back my Donna Duck," she demanded.

"Donna Duck, what a stupid name," said the big girl.

But she gave Alison her glove puppet.

"Look, Donna. These are my new friends," said Alison.

"Let me have my bouncy ball back," she said.

"It's a hopeless bouncer anyway!" said the boy from Number Six.

But he gave her the ball.

Alison threw the ball, high, high into the air.
"Look at the lovely colours!" she shouted.

Next door's dog rushed out onto the pavement, barking. Donna Duck barked back even louder and the dog ran away as fast as it could.

Alison opened the door.
"Come in," she said. "What sort of ice cream do you like?"

There was no answer.
There was no one there.

But Alison did not feel sad.

Not at all.